YOU AND YOUR CHILD
CHRISTMAS

Ray Gibson

Illustrated by Simone Wood, Sue Stitt
and Graham Round

Designed by Carol Law

Edited by Robyn Gee

Series editor: Jenny Tyler

Photography by Lesley Howling

Much of the pleasure of Christmas is in the anticipation and preparation. This book provides parents and children with lots of ideas for simple things to make together to get themselves in the festive mood. There are hanging decorations, table decorations and tree decorations; ideas for advent calendars, cards and presents and tasty things to eat. Besides introducing children to some Christmas traditions and helping them to play a part in the preparations, the activities in this book provide the context for a wealth of learning opportunities.

First published in 1991 by Usborne Publishing Ltd, Usborne House, 83-85 Saffron Hill, London EC1N 8RT, England. Copyright © 1991 Usborne Publishing Ltd. The name Usborne and the device ☙ are Trade Marks of Usborne Publishing Ltd. All rights reserved.
Printed in Belgium.

Christmas angel

You will need:
1 large doyley
round-ended scissors
stiff red paper
scrap of pink paper
cotton wool
paper clip
PVA glue
glue stick
yellow wool
sticky tape

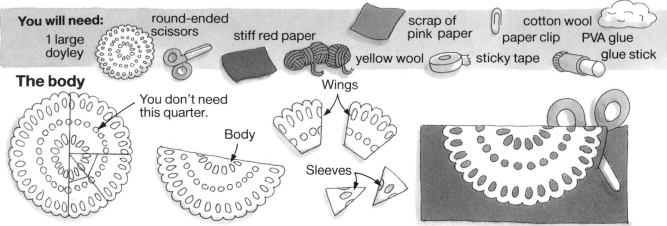

The body

Wings

Body

Sleeves

Draw lines on the doyley, as shown above. Cut along them to make two wings, sleeves and a body.

You don't need this quarter.

Spread glue on the back of the body piece and stick it onto red paper. When dry, cut round the edge of the doyley.

On the back, glue along half of the straight edge.

Snip across the top to leave a small hole.

Hold in place with a paper clip until it is dry.

Bend it into a cone shape, overlapping the glued edge and press it down firmly.

Fold a piece of pink paper and cut out two small hands.
   Glue them onto the ends of the sleeves. Leave them to dry.

Other ideas to try

Wise men

Instead of haloes give them kitchen paper headdresses.

Fairy

Give her a tinsel headdress and glue sequins over her dress and wings.

Angel mobile

Make several angels and hang them from a garden cane.

The join goes down the back of the body.

Glue the pointed end of the sleeves to the body, as shown.

2

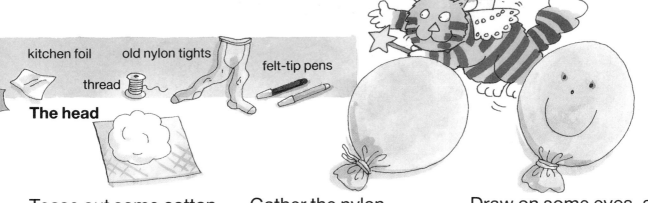

kitchen foil   old nylon tights

thread   felt-tip pens

The head

Tease out some cotton wool and roll it into a firm ball. Put it in the centre of a square cut from some nylon tights.

Gather the nylon around the cotton wool, twist the corners together and tie thread around them.

Draw on some eyes, a nose and a mouth with felt-tip pen.

Snip some wool into short pieces for hair. Put glue onto the head and press them on.

Push the bottom of the head firmly through the hole in the top of the cone. Fix it inside with sticky tape.

Cut out a circle of foil and glue it onto the back of the head as a halo.

Glue the wings to the back of the body, over the arms and hands.

Hint

• To make the wings really strong, you could stick them onto clear cellophane, before attaching them to the body.

3

Swedish hanging biscuits

You will need:

225 g (8 oz) plain flour

½ teaspoon bicarbonate of soda

115 g (4 oz) margarine

pinch of ground cloves

¾ teaspoon cinnamon

icing sugar

green and red glacé cherries

115 g (4 oz) dark brown sugar

¾ teaspoon ground ginger

1 egg white

cold water

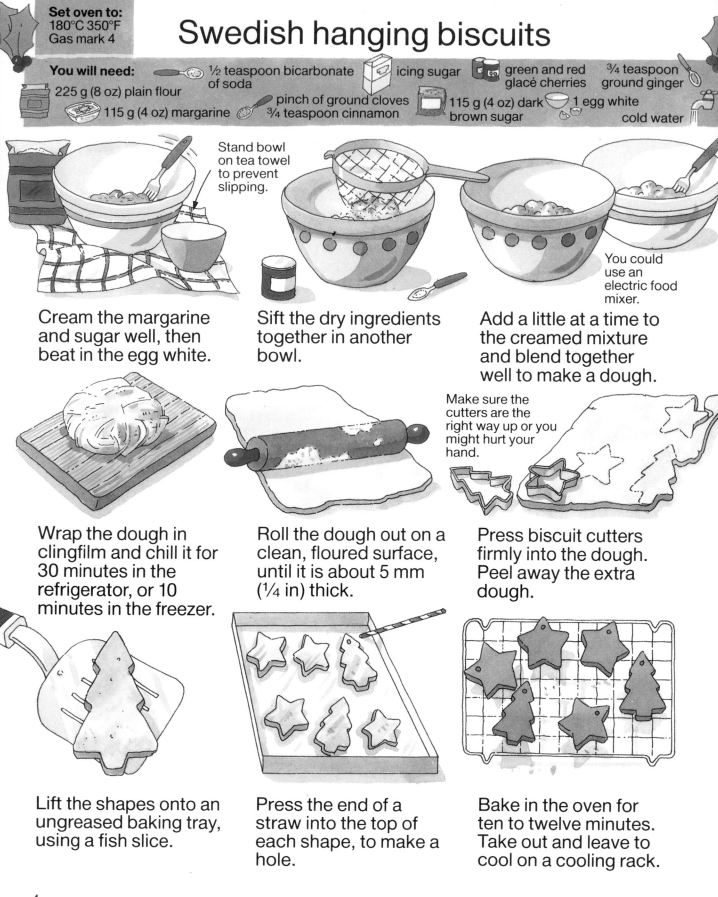

Stand bowl on tea towel to prevent slipping.

You could use an electric food mixer.

Cream the margarine and sugar well, then beat in the egg white.

Sift the dry ingredients together in another bowl.

Add a little at a time to the creamed mixture and blend together well to make a dough.

Make sure the cutters are the right way up or you might hurt your hand.

Wrap the dough in clingfilm and chill it for 30 minutes in the refrigerator, or 10 minutes in the freezer.

Roll the dough out on a clean, floured surface, until it is about 5 mm (¼ in) thick.

Press biscuit cutters firmly into the dough. Peel away the extra dough.

Lift the shapes onto an ungreased baking tray, using a fish slice.

Press the end of a straw into the top of each shape, to make a hole.

Bake in the oven for ten to twelve minutes. Take out and leave to cool on a cooling rack.

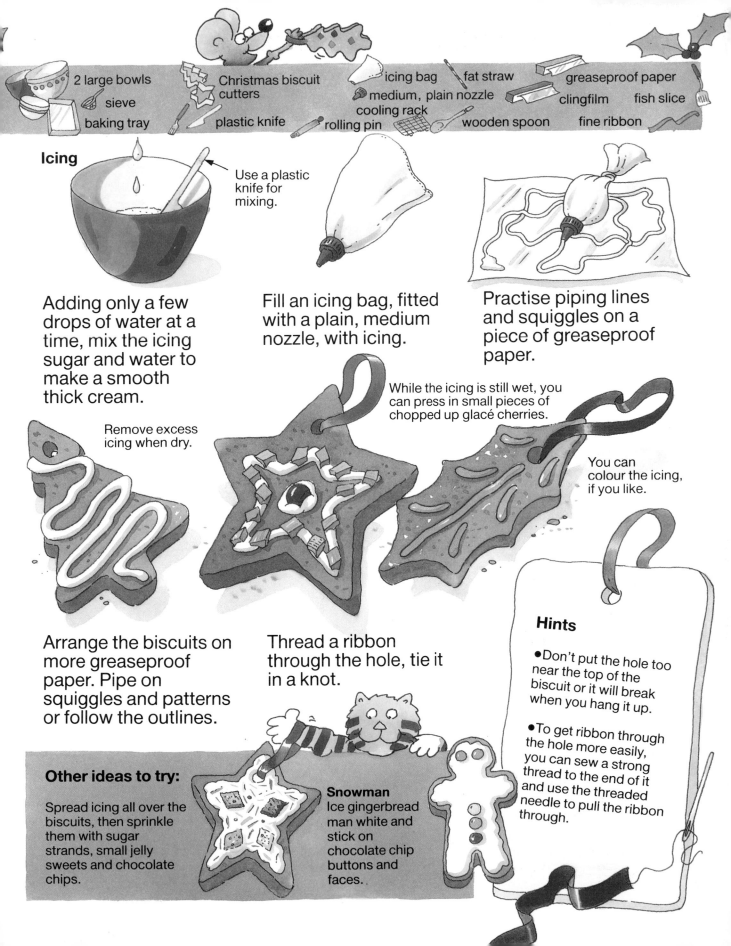

2 large bowls
Christmas biscuit cutters
icing bag
fat straw
greaseproof paper
sieve
medium, plain nozzle
clingfilm   fish slice
cooling rack
baking tray
plastic knife
rolling pin
wooden spoon
fine ribbon

Icing

Use a plastic knife for mixing.

Adding only a few drops of water at a time, mix the icing sugar and water to make a smooth thick cream.

Fill an icing bag, fitted with a plain, medium nozzle, with icing.

Practise piping lines and squiggles on a piece of greaseproof paper.

While the icing is still wet, you can press in small pieces of chopped up glacé cherries.

Remove excess icing when dry.

You can colour the icing, if you like.

Arrange the biscuits on more greaseproof paper. Pipe on squiggles and patterns or follow the outlines.

Thread a ribbon through the hole, tie it in a knot.

Hints

• Don't put the hole too near the top of the biscuit or it will break when you hang it up.

• To get ribbon through the hole more easily, you can sew a strong thread to the end of it and use the threaded needle to pull the ribbon through.

Other ideas to try:

Spread icing all over the biscuits, then sprinkle them with sugar strands, small jelly sweets and chocolate chips.

Snowman
Ice gingerbread man white and stick on chocolate chip buttons and faces.

Glitter garlands

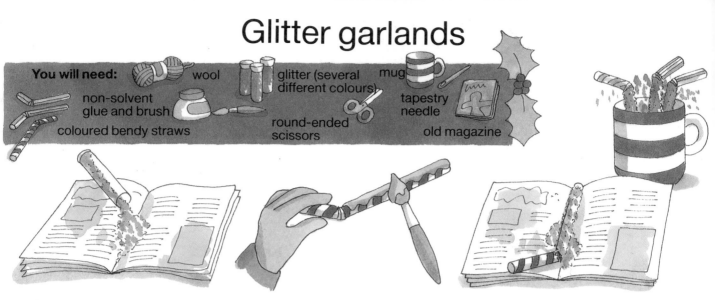

Open an old magazine out flat and pour glitter in a line down the centre fold.

Bend the short end of a straw and using it as a handle brush glue all over the long end.

Roll the straw in the glitter until it is covered. Stand it handle end up in a mug to dry.
Repeat this with several more straws.
Tip any excess glitter back into the container.

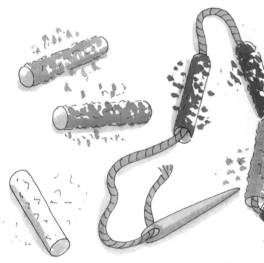

Snip the straws into pieces about 2 or 3 cm (1 in) long. Thread wool through them, using a blunt needle.

Secure the first 'bead' with a knot before continuing.

Warning

Take care to wash hands immediately after using glitter to avoid it going in eyes and mouths.

Hang in loops round the Christmas tree.

Other ideas

Instead of using glitter, wrap straws in strips of kitchen foil.

Secure the foil with sticky tape before snipping the straws.

Cut longer pieces and thread them three at a time to make triangle shapes, tying the ends together at the top.

Paper stockings

You will need:

non-solvent glue

round-ended scissors

scraps of tinsel

ribbon

small sweets

strong, bright Christmas paper

paper clips

gift wrap tape

ruler

felt-tip pens

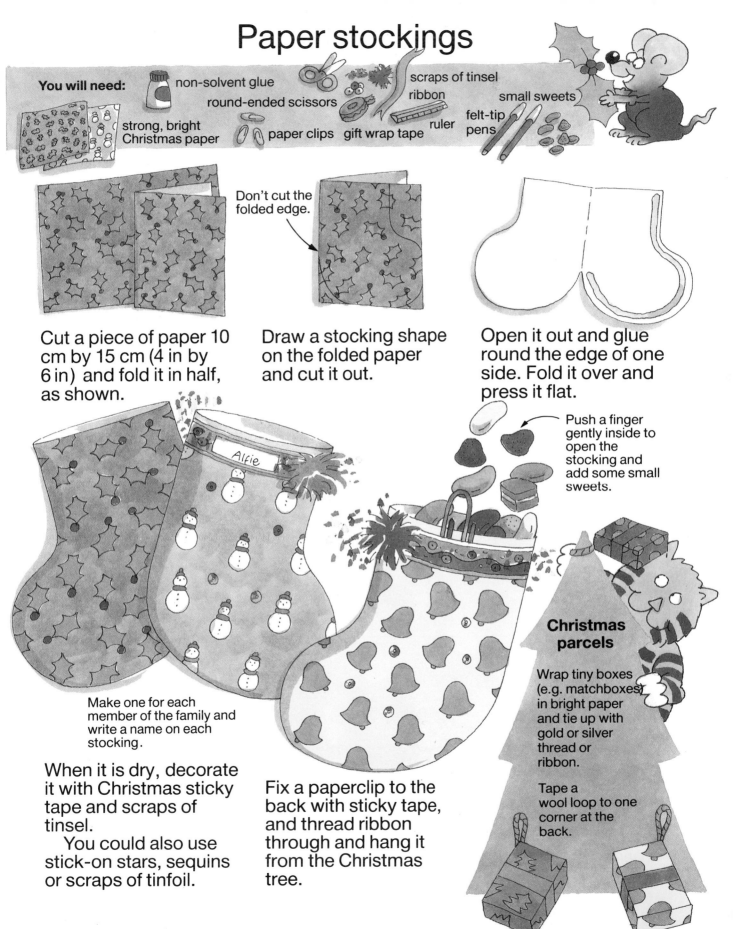

Cut a piece of paper 10 cm by 15 cm (4 in by 6 in) and fold it in half, as shown.

Don't cut the folded edge.

Draw a stocking shape on the folded paper and cut it out.

Open it out and glue round the edge of one side. Fold it over and press it flat.

Push a finger gently inside to open the stocking and add some small sweets.

Make one for each member of the family and write a name on each stocking.

When it is dry, decorate it with Christmas sticky tape and scraps of tinsel.

You could also use stick-on stars, sequins or scraps of tinfoil.

Fix a paperclip to the back with sticky tape, and thread ribbon through and hang it from the Christmas tree.

Christmas parcels

Wrap tiny boxes (e.g. matchboxes) in bright paper and tie up with gold or silver thread or ribbon.

Tape a wool loop to one corner at the back.

Candle in a pot

You will need: small plastic tub, small tinfoil dish, old newspaper, jug cold water, round-ended scissors, small piece yellow and orange felt, small Christmas decorations, plaster of paris, parcel ribbon, tinsel, candle, sticky tape, PVA glue, stick for mixing

Spread out some old newspaper to work on. Pour cold water into a plastic tub almost to the brim.

Add some plaster of paris and stir the mixture. It should feel like thick cream.

Add more water or plaster to get the right thickness.

Pour the mixture into a tinfoil dish.

Push a candle into the centre and hold it upright until it can stand by itself.

Quickly push decorations into the plaster around the base of the candle. Leave it to set.

Warning
Plaster of paris sets very quickly, so make sure you have everything you need to hand.

← felt flame

Tape tinsel around the rim of your dish.

Add a bow and a band made from parcel ribbon.

Cut out a yellow felt 'flame' and glue it to the wick.

Give the flame a centre made from orange felt.

Hints

- You can buy plaster of paris in most large chemists.

- Before you start you could brush your candle with glue and roll it in glitter.

- Instead of a candle you coud use a cardboard tube covered with crêpe paper.

- You could use playdough, instead of plaster of paris, if you prefer.

Warning
Liquid plaster will block the wastepipe if you pour it down the sink. Pour it into a plastic bag and allow it to set before throwing it away.

Robin on a log

You will need: round-ended scissors • tissue paper: 2 sheets brown, small piece red, small piece black, 1 sheet any colour • piece of log • yellow straw • 2 paper plates • holly and berries • pencil • spoon • PVA glue • plaster of paris • water

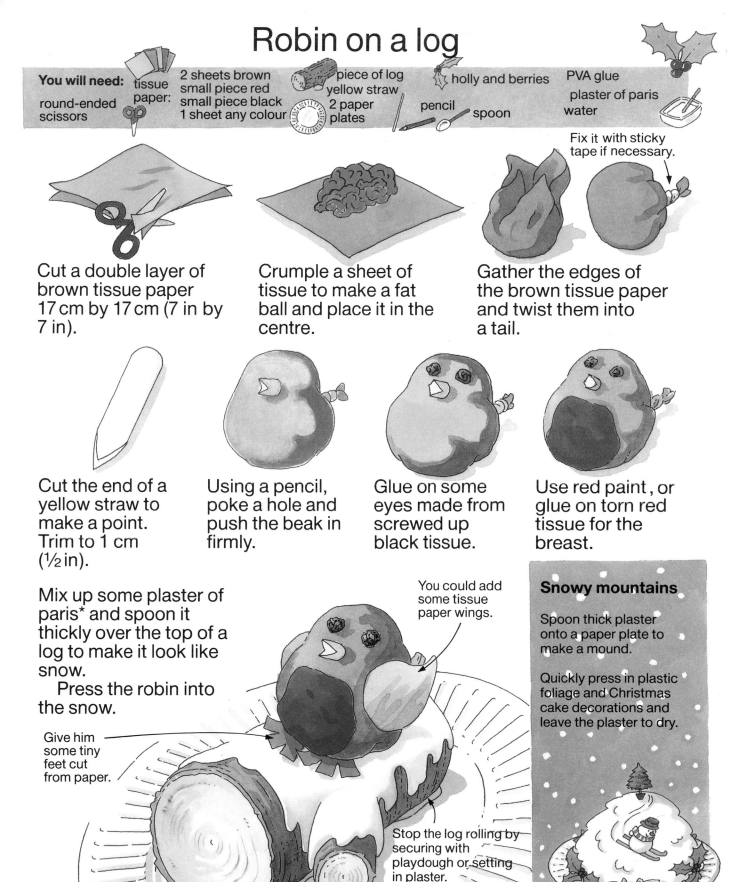

Cut a double layer of brown tissue paper 17 cm by 17 cm (7 in by 7 in).

Crumple a sheet of tissue to make a fat ball and place it in the centre.

Fix it with sticky tape if necessary.

Gather the edges of the brown tissue paper and twist them into a tail.

Cut the end of a yellow straw to make a point. Trim to 1 cm (½ in).

Using a pencil, poke a hole and push the beak in firmly.

Glue on some eyes made from screwed up black tissue.

Use red paint, or glue on torn red tissue for the breast.

Mix up some plaster of paris* and spoon it thickly over the top of a log to make it look like snow.
    Press the robin into the snow.

Give him some tiny feet cut from paper.

You could add some tissue paper wings.

Stop the log rolling by securing with playdough or setting in plaster.

Snowy mountains

Spoon thick plaster onto a paper plate to make a mound.

Quickly press in plastic foliage and Christmas cake decorations and leave the plaster to dry.

*See opposite page.

9

Marzipan fun

You will need:
100 g (4 oz) sifted icing sugar
small jug
100 g (4 oz) ground almonds
large mixing bowl
two teaspoonfuls of lemon juice
wooden spoon
1 egg white (see hints)
plastic bag

Making marzipan

Mix the icing sugar and ground almonds together in a mixing bowl, using a wooden spoon.

Beat the lemon juice and egg white together in a small jug, using a fork.

Add half the liquid to the bowl and mix well. Gradually add enough of the remaining liquid to turn the mixture into a stiff paste. Knead until smooth.

Hints

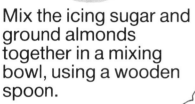

●The texture improves if it is kept in the refrigerator overnight.

●You can buy dried egg white, if you are worried about using uncooked egg white.

●A tea towel placed under the mixing bowl will help to prevent it slipping.

●If you want very strong colours you can paint food colour directly onto the marzipan, using a small brush. Leave it to dry.

Storing

Place in a polythene food bag and keep in the refrigerator. Use within seven days.

Adding colour

Pour drops of colour into small bowls and knead balls of marzipan in them until evenly coloured.

If the marzipan becomes too soft, add more icing sugar and mix well.

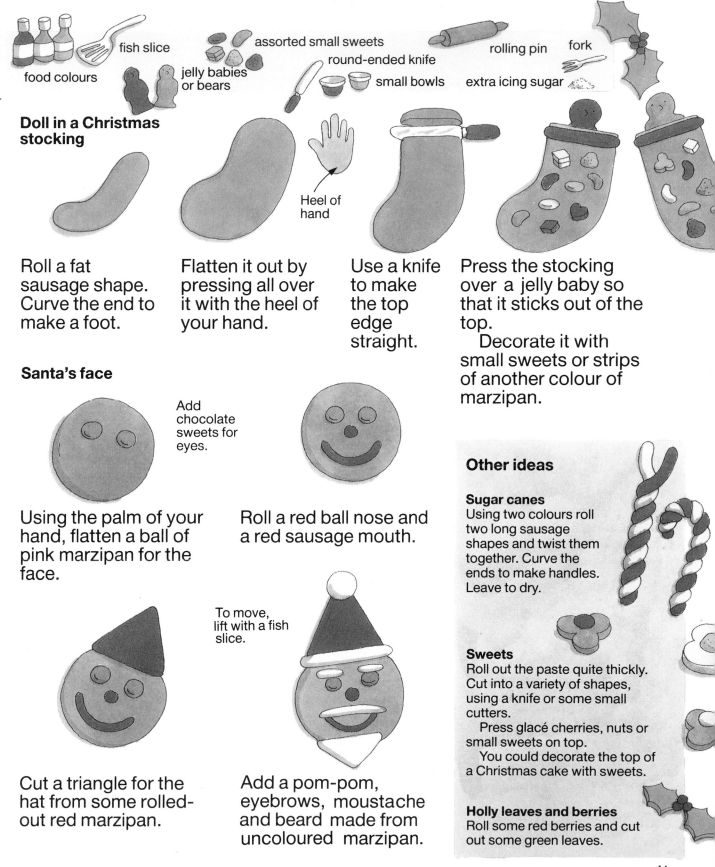

food colours

fish slice

jelly babies or bears

assorted small sweets

round-ended knife

small bowls

rolling pin

fork

extra icing sugar

Doll in a Christmas stocking

Heel of hand

Roll a fat sausage shape. Curve the end to make a foot.

Flatten it out by pressing all over it with the heel of your hand.

Use a knife to make the top edge straight.

Press the stocking over a jelly baby so that it sticks out of the top.

Decorate it with small sweets or strips of another colour of marzipan.

Santa's face

Add chocolate sweets for eyes.

Using the palm of your hand, flatten a ball of pink marzipan for the face.

Roll a red ball nose and a red sausage mouth.

To move, lift with a fish slice.

Cut a triangle for the hat from some rolled-out red marzipan.

Add a pom-pom, eyebrows, moustache and beard made from uncoloured marzipan.

Other ideas

Sugar canes
Using two colours roll two long sausage shapes and twist them together. Curve the ends to make handles. Leave to dry.

Sweets
Roll out the paste quite thickly. Cut into a variety of shapes, using a knife or some small cutters.

Press glacé cherries, nuts or small sweets on top.

You could decorate the top of a Christmas cake with sweets.

Holly leaves and berries
Roll some red berries and cut out some green leaves.

Mincemeat

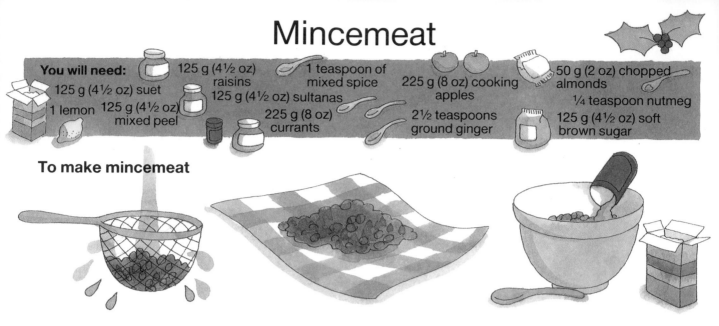

You will need: 125 g (4½ oz) suet · 1 lemon · 125 g (4½ oz) mixed peel · 125 g (4½ oz) raisins · 125 g (4½ oz) sultanas · 225 g (8 oz) currants · 1 teaspoon of mixed spice · 2½ teaspoons ground ginger · 225 g (8 oz) cooking apples · 50 g (2 oz) chopped almonds · ¼ teaspoon nutmeg · 125 g (4½ oz) soft brown sugar

To make mincemeat

Place the currants, raisins and sultanas in a sieve and wash them under the cold tap.

Shake the sieve well, then tip them onto a clean tea towel and pat them dry.

Tip them into a large bowl. Add sugar, spices, almonds, mixed peel and suet.

Cut the apples into halves, then quarters, then smaller segments.

Cut the peel from each segment and slice out the core from the centres.

You could use a food processor.

Put a few segments at a time onto a chopping board and chop them up finely. Add the apple to the dried fruit.

Wash the lemon and dry it with a tea towel.

With a fine grater, gently grate off the outer rind into a small bowl.

Cut the lemon in half and squeeze out all the juice.

Add the juice and rind to the large bowl.

Mix it up well using a wooden spoon. Leave the mixture covered for 24 hours.

12   *For vegetarians use vegetable suet.

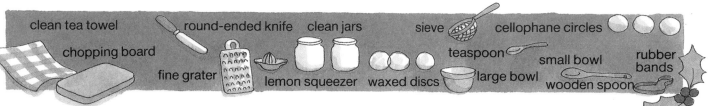

clean tea towel • round-ended knife • clean jars • sieve • cellophane circles • chopping board • fine grater • lemon squeezer • waxed discs • large bowl • teaspoon • small bowl • wooden spoon • rubber bands

To bottle

First you need to sterilize some jam jars by washing them in a dishwasher or using sterilizing solution (see Hint box).

Fill the jars with mincemeat then place a waxed disc on top. Cover either with a screw top or with a cellophane circle secured with a rubber band.

Leave for at least two weeks before using.

Hint

• You can buy sterilizing solution from chemists. To use it follow the instructions on the bottle or packet.

To mum
Love from
Carol
x

If you want to gift wrap your mincemeat cut a circle of Christmas paper to cover the cellophane. Hold it in place with a ribbon. Stick on a gummed Christmas label.

Merry Christmas

Sadie

Mincemeat munchies

Christmas stars
Using a large star-shaped cutter, cut star shapes from rolled out shortcrust pastry about 3 mm (⅛ in) thick.

Place a little mincemeat in the centre of a star. Brush the edges of the pastry with milk. Place a second star on top to seal it. Glaze with a whole beaten egg.

To decorate snip the top of the pastry with scissors.

Bake on a greased tray at GM 6, 200°C, 400°F for about 15 minutes.

Warning

The mincemeat stays hot after the pastry has cooled down.

Christmas crackers

Place 1 teaspoon of mincemeat on an oblong of pastry about 8 cm by 12 cm (3 in by 5 in).

Brush one long edge with milk to seal it, then roll up the pastry.

With the seam underneath, pinch it into a cracker shape.

Add a small pastry decoration. Glaze and bake, as above.

Use a fish slice to move pastry shapes.

Paper cascade

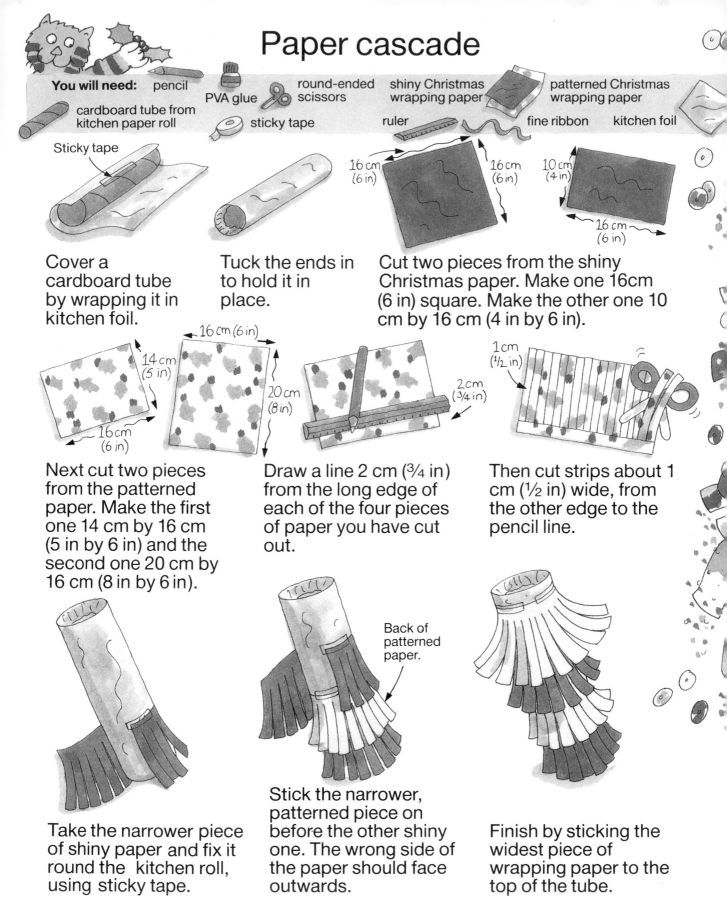

You will need: pencil, PVA glue, round-ended scissors, shiny Christmas wrapping paper, patterned Christmas wrapping paper, cardboard tube from kitchen paper roll, sticky tape, ruler, fine ribbon, kitchen foil

Sticky tape

Cover a cardboard tube by wrapping it in kitchen foil.

Tuck the ends in to hold it in place.

16 cm (6 in)   16 cm (6 in)   10 cm (4 in)   16 cm (6 in)

Cut two pieces from the shiny Christmas paper. Make one 16cm (6 in) square. Make the other one 10 cm by 16 cm (4 in by 6 in).

16 cm (6 in)   14 cm (5 in)   16 cm (6 in)   20 cm (8 in)

Next cut two pieces from the patterned paper. Make the first one 14 cm by 16 cm (5 in by 6 in) and the second one 20 cm by 16 cm (8 in by 6 in).

2 cm (¾ in)

Draw a line 2 cm (¾ in) from the long edge of each of the four pieces of paper you have cut out.

1 cm (½ in)

Then cut strips about 1 cm (½ in) wide, from the other edge to the pencil line.

Take the narrower piece of shiny paper and fix it round the kitchen roll, using sticky tape.

Back of patterned paper.

Stick the narrower, patterned piece on before the other shiny one. The wrong side of the paper should face outwards.

Finish by sticking the widest piece of wrapping paper to the top of the tube.

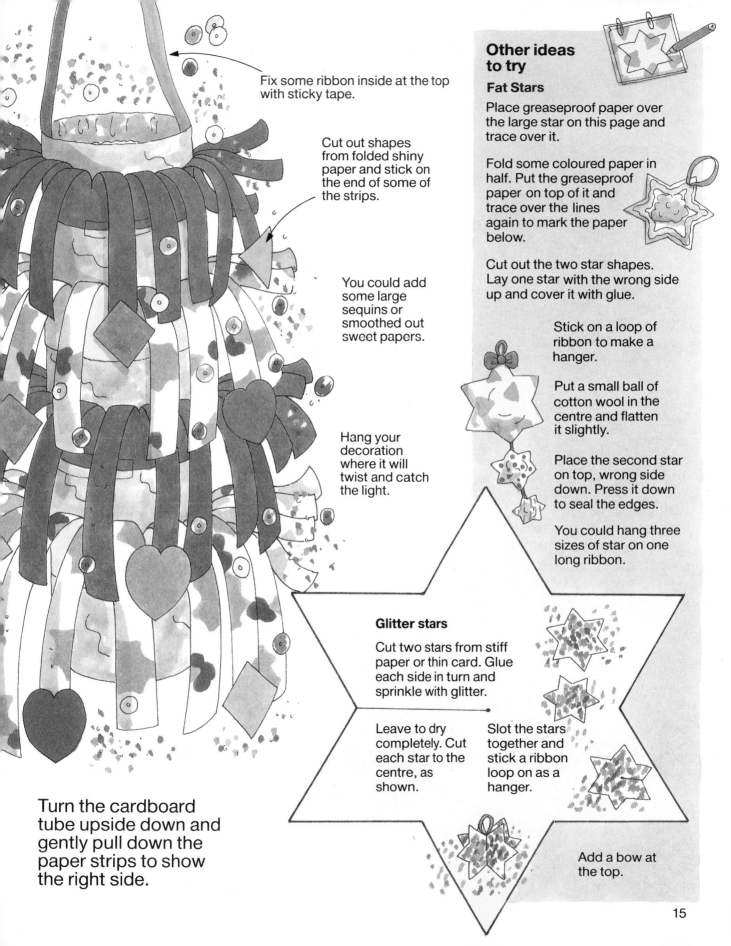

Fix some ribbon inside at the top with sticky tape.

Cut out shapes from folded shiny paper and stick on the end of some of the strips.

You could add some large sequins or smoothed out sweet papers.

Hang your decoration where it will twist and catch the light.

Turn the cardboard tube upside down and gently pull down the paper strips to show the right side.

Other ideas to try

Fat Stars

Place greaseproof paper over the large star on this page and trace over it.

Fold some coloured paper in half. Put the greaseproof paper on top of it and trace over the lines again to mark the paper below.

Cut out the two star shapes. Lay one star with the wrong side up and cover it with glue.

Stick on a loop of ribbon to make a hanger.

Put a small ball of cotton wool in the centre and flatten it slightly.

Place the second star on top, wrong side down. Press it down to seal the edges.

You could hang three sizes of star on one long ribbon.

Glitter stars

Cut two stars from stiff paper or thin card. Glue each side in turn and sprinkle with glitter.

Leave to dry completely. Cut each star to the centre, as shown.

Slot the stars together and stick a ribbon loop on as a hanger.

Add a bow at the top.

Gingerbread house

You will need:
290 g (11 oz) self-raising flour
1½ tablespoons ground ginger
½ tablespoon cinnamon
85 g (3 oz) butter
110 g (4 oz) castor sugar
1 egg
60 ml (2 fl oz) golden syrup
1 tablespoon black treacle

sieve
measuring jug
round-ended knife
large bowl
tablespoon
clingfilm

Stage 1: Making the gingerbread dough

Sift the flour and spices into a large bowl. Stir in the castor sugar with a spoon.

Cut the butter into small pieces. Rub it into the flour mixture with your fingers.

Measure the golden syrup into a measuring jug. Add the treacle and an egg. Mix well.

Make a well in the centre of the flour mixture. Add all the liquid at once.

Mix to a dough with a knife.

Wrap the dough in clingfilm and refrigerate it for 30 minutes.

Stage 2: Making the base and roof

You will need: plastic ruler, greaseproof paper, pencil, swiss roll tin, fish-slice, flour, rolling pin

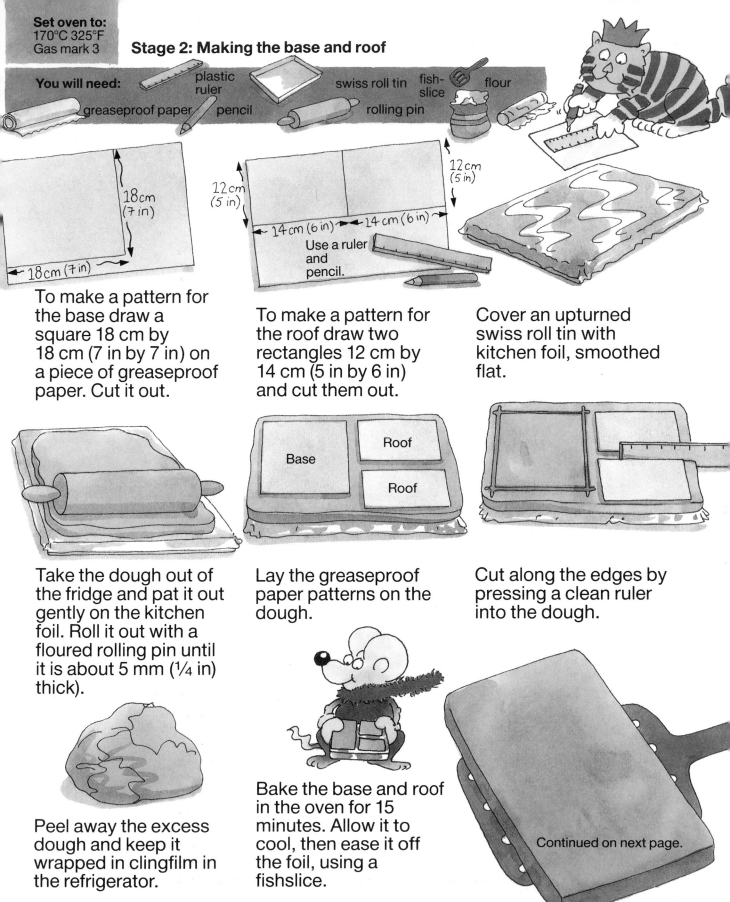

To make a pattern for the base draw a square 18 cm by 18 cm (7 in by 7 in) on a piece of greaseproof paper. Cut it out.

To make a pattern for the roof draw two rectangles 12 cm by 14 cm (5 in by 6 in) and cut them out.

Cover an upturned swiss roll tin with kitchen foil, smoothed flat.

Take the dough out of the fridge and pat it out gently on the kitchen foil. Roll it out with a floured rolling pin until it is about 5 mm (¼ in) thick).

Lay the greaseproof paper patterns on the dough.

Cut along the edges by pressing a clean ruler into the dough.

Peel away the excess dough and keep it wrapped in clingfilm in the refrigerator.

Bake the base and roof in the oven for 15 minutes. Allow it to cool, then ease it off the foil, using a fishslice.

Continued on next page.

17

Stage 3: Icing and decorating your house

You will need:
225 g (8 oz) icing sugar
egg white powder
bowl
whisk
water
sugar strands
cakeboard
spoon
assortment of different coloured sweets and cake decorations

Put the short sides at the top and bottom.

Mix up some egg white powder with water* and whisk in icing sugar to make a fairly thick paste.

Put the base of the house on a cakeboard. Spread some icing over it and sprinkle it with sugar strands.

Prop the two roof pieces against each other, 3 cm (1 in) from the edge of the base and 1 cm (½ in) from the back.

Dribble on icing icicles, using a spoon, or pipe it on with an icing bag.

Hold them together while you dribble icing thickly from a spoon along the top, to seal them together.

Hints

- If the icing hardens too quickly, dip the sweets in the bowl of icing and glue them on.

- If you haven't got a cakeboard, cover a wooden board or tray and use sticky tape to hold it in position.

Allow the icing to harden a little, then spread more icing over the roof to cover it.

Press sweets or cake decorations into the icing to decorate the roof.

*Follow the instructions on the packet to make the equivalent of one fresh egg white.

Stage 4: Making the witch and the children

You will need:

white marzipan

small gingerbread man cutters

round-ended knife

pink, red and blue food colouring

3 saucers

rolling pin

Pink ball for head.

White body and arms.

Pink balls for hands

Red skirt. Press in folds with a knife.

Walking stick.

Colour some marzipan by kneading balls of it in saucers containing a few drops of food colouring.

Roll and cut out the pieces shown above.

Red ball brooch.

Blue shawl.

Press in eyes and a mouth.

Give her a round red nose.

Stand witch in doorway.

Press the pieces together and wrap the shawl round her.

Gingerbread children

Roll out the dough left over when you cut out the base and roof.
Use flour to stop the rolling pin sticking.

Cut out two children with gingerbread man cutters. Use a knife if you don't have cutters.

Bake them in the oven for 15 minutes.

Hold the children in position with icing glue.

Nativity scene

You will need:
coloured tissue paper
round-ended scissors
clingfilm
a cardboard tube from a toilet roll 10 cm (4 in) high for each figure
plastic tray or wooden board
large bowl warm water
ruler
pencil

Joseph

You could cut several at once.

Cut some tissue paper squares, about 24 cm (9 in) square.

Stand a cardboard tube on a plastic tray or board covered with clingfilm.

Dip a tissue paper square into a bowl of warm water. Lift it out and allow it to drip for a few seconds.

Drape it over the tube and arrange it in folds. Dry in a warm place, or in a microwave for 3 or 4 minutes.

The head

Leave a long tail.

Secure with sticky tape.

Crumple some tissue paper into a ball and wrap it in a tissue paper square. Gather the corners together and twist.

Poke a large hole in the tissue at the top of the tube. Put the base of the head in and fix with tape inside.

Arms

Cut three pieces of tissue about 8 cm by 16 cm (3 in by 6 in).

Crumple two of the pieces and lay them on top of the third piece.

Roll up the third piece, twisting it firmly at both ends.

Pinch the middle flat, then twist two or three times.

sticky tape · parcel tape or ribbon · drinking straws · Continued on next page.

felt-tip pens · PVA glue · inside of a large matchbox · breadknife

Use felt-tips to draw on eyes, a nose and a mouth.

Attach the ends of the arms to the body with sticky tape.

Roll up and twist some tissue paper to make a belt. Fix it on with sticky tape.

Cut a piece of tissue for a cloak. Wet it and drape it around the head. Leave to dry.

Baby Jesus

Wrap a piece of crumpled tissue inside some pink tissue. Tape it to one end of a tissue paper sausage.

Cut a long strip of paper, 2 cm (¾ in) wide. Wrap the baby in it, starting with the head. Fix it with sticky tape. Draw on a face and place it in the crib.

Crib

Cut strips of yellow tissue for straw. Arrange it inside a large matchbox.

Kneeling Mary

Cut a cardboard tube in half, using a breadknife. Drape her robe and cloak behind her.

Cut a piece of straw to make a staff.

21

2 bottle tops · **egg box** · **sequins** · **feather** · **cotton wool** · **kitchen foil** · **PVA glue** · **foil sweet wrapper** · **painted pasta shell**

The three kings

Headdresses

Cut out a section of egg carton. Cover it with kitchen foil.

Trim it with twisted foil and tissue.

Fix sticky tape round base of headdress. Place on head over cloak.

Cover a bottle top with foil. Stick on a small feather or piece of tissue.

Wrap a turban made from twisted tissue paper round the head. Secure it with sticky tape.

Gifts

Painted pasta shell with crumpled foil jewel on top.

Crumpled tissue inside a foil sweet wrapper. Glue on sequins.

Bottle top covered in kitchen foil with gummed paper star stuck on.

Belts

Use shiny parcel ribbon, or twisted kitchen foil.
   You could twist kitchen foil and tissue together.

Shepherds

Use brown, grey and black tissue with plain headbands.

Shepherd's crook

Roll a twisted length of kitchen foil with black or brown tissue. Bend it into shape.

Lambs

Roll cotton wool into sausage shapes for the bodies.
For the heads, wrap crumpled pieces of tissue, inside black tissue rectangles. Twist the corners to make ears. Glue onto the bodies.

Christmas party games

Christmas puddings

Two or more players

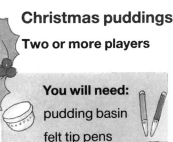

You will need:

- pudding basin
- felt tip pens
- number dice
- 1 sheet of paper for each player
- sultanas
- egg cup

Place the sultanas in the pudding basin and the dice in the egg cup.

Each player draws a large outline of a Christmas pudding on their paper.

The players agree on how many times they will each throw the dice. They then take it in turns to throw it.

Whatever number comes up is the number of sultanas you can take from the pudding bowl and put in your pudding.

The winner is the one with the most sultanas at the end.

Jingle bells

Two or more players

One person goes out of the room and the others choose an object they can see.

The person comes back in and begins to move about the room. The other players chant "Jingle bells" very quietly if they are not near the object, getting louder as they get nearer until the object is found.

Hint

For "Christmas puddings" instead of a dice you could use six chocolate coins. Stick a gummed star or label on one side of each.

Toss in the air from a small bowl. The number of stars showing when they land is the number of sultanas you can take.

Christmas tree

Any number of players

One player is the questioner. She asks the other players questions.

Whatever the question they must always answer "A Christmas tree". If you giggle when you answer you are out.

Father Christmas

At least three players

One person is the "loader", the others are all Father Christmases.

The loader has a heap of soft toys, boxes and light, unbreakable household objects. She gives each player in turn one item to hold.

The first player to drop something is out.

The last one left in is the real Father Christmas.

Glittery bell card

You will need: stiff paper · old Christmas card · old newspaper · paperclips · PVA glue · glitter · pencil · envelope · damp cloth · round-ended scissors · saucer · brush

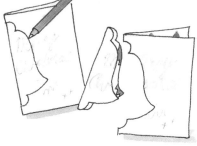

Find an envelope and cut and fold some paper to make a card to fit inside it.

To make a bell stencil draw half a bell shape down the folded edge of an old Christmas card.
   Cut the shape out carefully, saving both pieces.

Open out the card you have made. Lay your stencil on the front of it and fix it in position with paperclips.

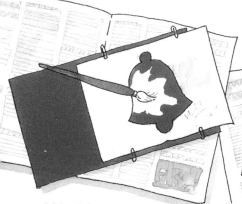

If you use a shiny Christmas card you can wipe your stencil with a damp cloth and use it again.

Working on newspaper, spread glue thinly over the cut-out area of the stencil. Remove the stencil carefully.

Sprinkle glitter over the glued area. Tip the excess off into a saucer to use again.

Leave the card to lie flat until the glue is completely dry.

Silhouette card

Use the bell shape cut from the Christmas card above.

Hold it in position in the centre of a card. Dab around the outline with a sponge dipped in white paint, to make a snow effect.

Lift it off carefully. Decorate the bell with sequins, gummed stars, foil scraps or narrow ribbon.

Decorated tree cards

You will need: scraps of coloured paper · doyley (white, silver or gold) · stick-on gold and silver stars · glitter · narrow parcel ribbon · stiff paper · glue stick

Cut tree shapes from stiff paper and decorate them. Write your message on the back, or stick them onto folded cards.

Stick stars on top.

Glitter outline

Stick lengths of narrow parcel ribbon to criss-cross tree. Trim it at the edges.

Glue on screwed-up scraps of coloured paper.

Cut a tree from a doyley. Glue it over a bright colour to make a lacy effect.

Card hanger

Cut a length of bright ribbon.

Glue a cut-out picture from an old Christmas card near the top.

Hang from a small nail, or pin onto a picture rail using drawing pins.

Use paper clips to fix cards onto the ribbon.

Cut a "V" shape from the bottom of the ribbon

Other ideas

Pop-up card

Glue a small piece of folded card inside a folded card, matching the centre folds.

Glue a small cut-out picture from an old Christmas card on one side of the tab.

Collage card

Use cut-out pictures from old Christmas cards, wrapping paper and magazines.

Glue them onto prepared cards, overlapping the pictures.

25

Sponge print Christmas card

You will need: sponge cleaning cloth about 5mm (¼ in) thick · thin cardboard · PVA glue · round coin · thick paintbrush · Christmas tree biscuit cutter (see hints) · strong round-ended scissors · plastic bottle tops · felt-tip pen

To make your sponge printing blocks

Prepare some cards for printing on, by cutting and folding paper to fit in your envelopes.

Cut a piece of cardboard the same size as your sponge cloth.

Working on old newspapers, spread the cardboard with glue and then press the sponge firmly onto it.

Turn the sponge side downwards and draw round your Christmas tree biscuit cutter (see hints) onto the cardboard.

Leave until completely dry, then cut out the tree shape with scissors. Cut it out roughly first, then trim it. Save the leftover pieces.

To make a handle, glue a bottle top to the cardboard side of the tree shape.

Snow printing block

Using leftover pieces of sponge and cardboard snip small shapes.

Glue them card side down onto another piece of backing card.

Glue a bottle top handle on the back.

Sun printing block

Draw round a coin, or other round object onto a piece of the leftover card and sponge.

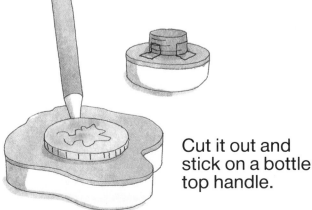

Cut it out and stick on a bottle top handle.

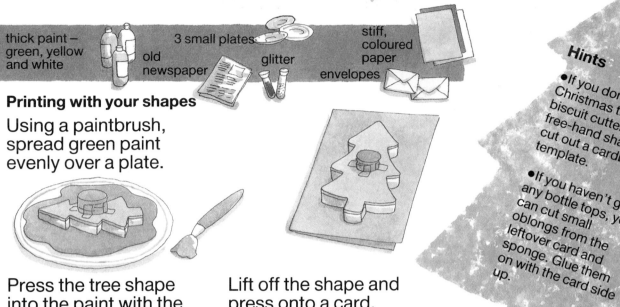

thick paint —
green, yellow
and white

old
newspaper

3 small plates

glitter

stiff,
coloured
paper

envelopes

Hints

- If you don't have a Christmas tree biscuit cutter draw a free-hand shape or cut out a cardboard template.

- If you haven't got any bottle tops, you can cut small oblongs from the leftover card and sponge. Glue them on with the card side up.

Printing with your shapes

Using a paintbrush, spread green paint evenly over a plate.

Press the tree shape into the paint with the sponge side down. Move it gently from side to side to make sure it is well covered.

Lift off the shape and press onto a card. Press the edges down well, using fingers if necessary. Peel off carefully.

Put yellow paint on a plate and press your round printer into it to print a sun.

Use white paint for your snow print.

You could sprinkle your card with glitter before the paint dries.

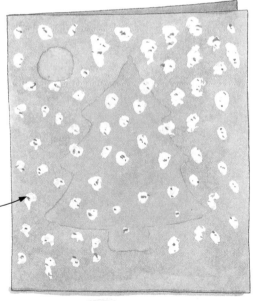

Snowman

Cut cardboard shapes for the hat, head and body and scarf.

Add painted eyes, nose and mouth.

Gift tags

Make small cards to print on.

Tie with decorative parcel string or use a hole punch to make a

hole in the top left corner. Thread with parcel string.

27

Nodding reindeer

You will need: sticky tape · pencil about 12 cm (5 in) long · PVA glue · ballpoint pen · scissors · cereal box · playdough · 2 twigs · small box about 4 cm by 8 cm (1½ in by 3 in) · large paintbrush · white paper · old newspaper · felt-tip pen · thread · brown poster paint

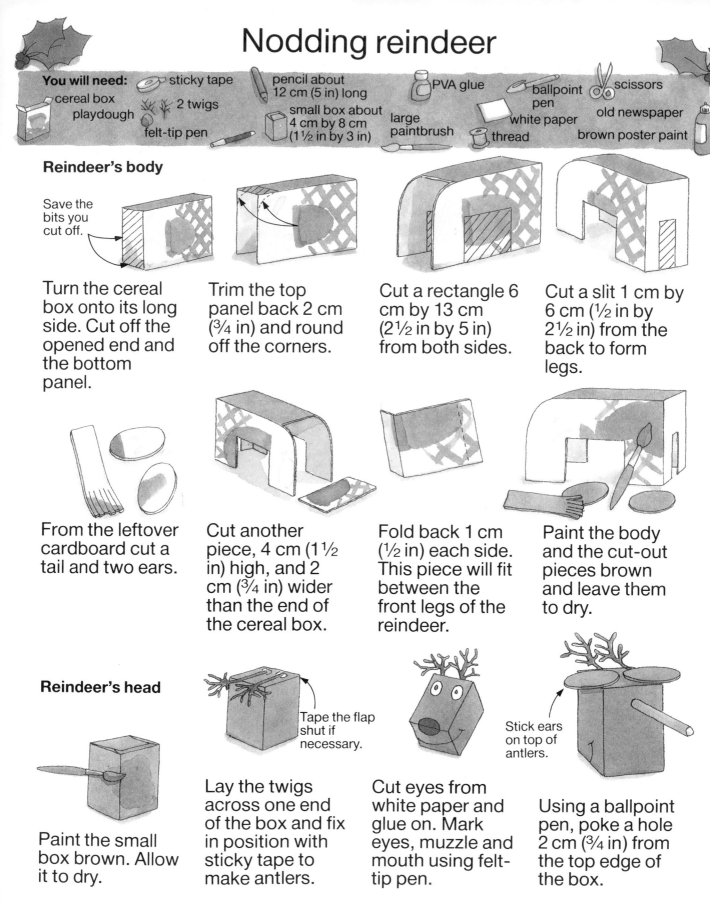

Reindeer's body

Save the bits you cut off.

Turn the cereal box onto its long side. Cut off the opened end and the bottom panel.

Trim the top panel back 2 cm (¾ in) and round off the corners.

Cut a rectangle 6 cm by 13 cm (2½ in by 5 in) from both sides.

Cut a slit 1 cm by 6 cm (½ in by 2½ in) from the back to form legs.

From the leftover cardboard cut a tail and two ears.

Cut another piece, 4 cm (1½ in) high, and 2 cm (¾ in) wider than the end of the cereal box.

Fold back 1 cm (½ in) each side. This piece will fit between the front legs of the reindeer.

Paint the body and the cut-out pieces brown and leave them to dry.

Reindeer's head

Paint the small box brown. Allow it to dry.

Lay the twigs across one end of the box and fix in position with sticky tape to make antlers.

Tape the flap shut if necessary.

Cut eyes from white paper and glue on. Mark eyes, muzzle and mouth using felt-tip pen.

Stick ears on top of antlers.

Using a ballpoint pen, poke a hole 2 cm (¾ in) from the top edge of the box.

To fix the head and body together

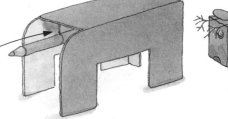

Leave the ends at least 5 cm (2 in) long.

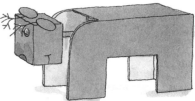

Leave about 2 cm (¾ in) between the pencil and the tape.

Tie a thread round a pencil. You should be able to slide the loop up and down the pencil.

Suspend the pencil by taping the threads to the inside top centre of the body.

Poke the pencil into the hole in the back of the head.

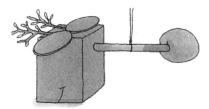

Press a ball of playdough onto the other end of the pencil, so that the head swings up a little.

If the head is too low add more playdough, if too high take a little off.

Slide the pencil through the loop if necessary, to adjust the angle of the head. The reindeer should nod freely when you tap his head.

Glue the tail onto the back.

The front panel goes between the front legs.

Finishing off

Put glue on the end of the tail and stick it onto the body.

Glue the sides of the front panel and stick it between the front legs to strengthen them.

Chocolate money tree

You will need:

- 24 chocolate coins
- bare, twiggy branch about 50 cm (20 in) long
- 24 sticky price labels
- wide ribbon
- sticky tape
- old newspaper
- white poster paint
- plastic flowerpot (at least 9 cm (4 in) high)
- silver glitter
- kitchen foil
- plastic knife
- thick brush
- scissors
- jug of water
- plaster of paris
- felt-tip pen
- pebbles
- large plastic tub
- fine string

Spread out some old newspaper to work on.

If it tears repair it with sticky tape.

Line a plastic flowerpot with tinfoil to make it water tight. Put some pebbles at the bottom.

Wrap the outside of the pot in tinfoil. Tuck it under the base and over the rim.

Push a branch firmly into the pot between the pebbles until it touches the bottom.

Use a plastic knife.

In a plastic tub mix up some plaster of paris* with water until it is smooth and creamy.

Pour the plaster of paris round the branch, over the pebbles. Hold the branch upright until the plaster sets.

Paint the branches white. Sprinkle them with glitter as you go, before the paint dries.

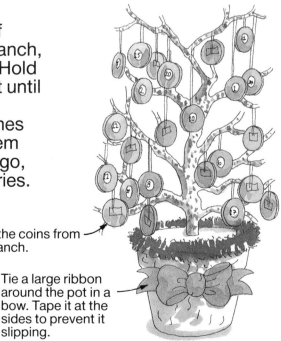

Hang the coins from the branch.

Tie a large ribbon around the pot in a bow. Tape it at the sides to prevent it slipping.

14

Cut some string into pieces about 15 cm (6 in) long. Tape the ends of each piece to a coin to make a loop.

Number some sticky labels from one to 24. Peel them off and stick them onto the coins.

Snip off one coin each day from December 1 until Christmas Eve. You could replace the coins with small ornaments, ribbon bows or pictures cut from old Christmas cards.

*For advice on using plaster of paris see page 8.

Advent parcel

You will need:

thin cardboard · pencil · 4 egg boxes · round-ended scissors · PVA glue · sticky tape · large sheet red tissue paper · felt-tip pen · 24 sticky price labels · 24 small sweets or presents · Christmas sticky tape · large parcel label · string · large ribbon bow

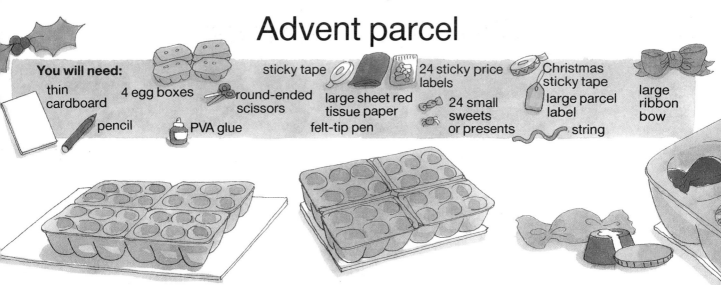

Cut the tops off four egg boxes. Glue the underside of the bottom halves and place them on a sheet of thin cardboard.

Trim the card around the edges. Tape across the joins between the boxes.

Fill each section with a small sweet or toy (see below for ideas).

Brush glue along the tops of the egg boxes. Lay the tissue paper across them and press gently to the glued areas.

Tuck the overlapping tissue underneath. Turn the boxes over carefully and tape the tissue down.

Add a ribbon bow and a label.

Stick Christmas tape over the tissue paper, where the boxes join.

Hint

- If you have not got any sticky labels cut up some gummed paper squares.

To hang it up, knot both ends of a piece of string and tape it to the back of the parcel.

Number some sticky labels from one to 24 and stick one over each compartment in a random order.

From December 1 open one section each day by poking the tissue with a pencil.

Ideas for filling parcel: sweets · plastic ring or necklace · plastic spider · hairslide · soap shape · balloons · small rubber ball · badge · chocolate coin · paper hat · small coin · toy watch

Parents' notes

Gather together everything you will need for a project before you start, checking off each item with your child from the panels at the top of the pages.

Below are a few notes about some of the materials and equipment you will need.

Scissors

When working with young children it is always best to use round-ended scissors for safety. If you use sharp scissors at all, put them out of reach immediately after you have used them.

Glue

PVA (polyvinyl acetate) is the best glue to use for most of the projects. It is white, but dries transparent. Protect clothing with aprons and wash brushes out carefully after use. Don't use solvent-based glues.

Paints

Poster paint has good covering power. When covering large areas use small adult decorating brushes.

Breadknife

This is the best thing to use to cut through cardboard tubes, boxes etc. Use a sawing action and protect work surfaces with a thick layer of old newspaper.

Sticky tape

When you need to use several pieces cut them all at once and attach them lightly to the edge of your work surface for easy use.

Patterned or shiny Christmas tape is useful for decorating things.

Mixing containers

Use plastic icecream or margarine tubs for mixing plaster or watering down paint.

Glitter

When using glitter sprinkle it directly from the tube. Tip off the excess onto a piece of paper which has been folded in half then opened out. Refold the paper and pour the excess glitter back into the tube.

Plaster of paris

This can be bought from large chemists' shops.

Mix it slowly in a large tub so that the powder does not puff out.

To get rid of excess plaster, pour it into a plastic bag and wait for it to set before putting it in the bin.

Decorations

Bits of gold or glittery braid

Non-flammable tinsel

White, gold or silver doylies

Sequins

Beads

Coloured string

Scraps of felt

Cotton wool

Make sure that any tree decorations you buy for trimming are nonbreakable.

Paper and cardboard

The following types will come in handy: Christmas wrapping paper – new or used

Foil-backed paper – avoid the plastic kind, it's hard to handle.

Old Christmas cards

Kitchen foil – covers large areas well

Crêpe paper

Sweet wrappers – foil and cellophane

Cereal cardboard

Greaseproof paper – for tracing

Tissue paper

Ribbon
Florists' ribbon is inexpensive and curls well.